Tales of Court and Castle

Joan Bodger

Illustrated by Mark Lang

Tundra Books

Published in Canada by Tundra Books,
481 University Avenue, Toronto, Ontario M5G 2E9

Published in the United States by Tundra Books of Northern New York,
P.O. Box 1030, Plattsburgh, New York 12901

Library of Congress Control Number: 2002101149

National Library of Canada Cataloguing in Publication

Bodger, Joan
  Tales of court and castle

ISBN 0-88776-614-5

  I. Lang, Mark   II. Title.

PS8553.O44T34 2003   jC813'.54   C2002-900852-2
PZ8.1.B5882Ta 2003

We acknowledge the financial support of the Government of Canada
through the Book Publishing Industry Development Program and that of the
Government of Ontario through the Ontario Media Development
Corporation's Ontario Book Initiative. We further acknowledge the support
of the Canada Council for the Arts and the Ontario Arts Council for our
publishing program.

Design: Terri Nimmo

Printed and bound in Canada

1 2 3 4 5 6   08 07 06 05 04 03

CONTENTS

INTRODUCTION

by Ken Setterington

I have been pelted by rain, snow, and sleet, standing on
the site of an ancient castle in Cornwall, while Joan
Bodger told the story of Tristan's youth. At the fireside of
a fourteenth-century thatch-roofed inn, I've listened in
tears to her tell of Tristan's death. The first time I heard
the stories I was new to storytelling, learning the art
from Joan over twenty years ago. The last time I heard
them in her voice, she was close to death herself. She
was about to leave Toronto for Tofino, at the shore of the
Pacific – the last sight this admiral's daughter wished to
see. Though she was weak, she went to a Thousand and
One Nights of Storytelling to tell, for one last time, the
story of Tristan. The audience was transported by this
Joan in all her power, passing on tales so old that their
sources are as dim and foggy as a British twilight.

When you read these stories, think of the voices of the storytellers and of the listeners who came before you.

Imagine a cold, long December night eight hundred years ago. The lords and ladies have assembled, and the storyteller has taken his place in the middle of the great hall. It is quiet, or as quiet as it can be with the dogs rustling in the rushes underfoot and the wind seeping in around the tapestries that hang on the stone walls. The stories are of chivalrous deeds, treachery, and love.

Perhaps a servant was listening that night as he passed the tankards of ale. He may have taken that story, made it his own, and told it to his brothers and sisters around a peat fire on his rare day at home. One of them may have heard another version from a passing traveler at the summer fair. Years later, the different accounts may have melted into one as someone tells the tale on a trading ship plying the sea.

Each of these stories has had a life, has been told hundreds of times and sifted through a thousand sieves. What you will find here are the stories as Joan Bodger told them. Joan was a remarkable woman. Born in 1923, the daughter of an admiral, she and her sisters grew up in one rough port after another. The constant in her life was stories, both family stories and the rich lore of her British heritage. Her life was as colorful as any tale she told. She was by turns a decoder in the US army during World War II, the founder of the first Head Start program in New York State, a librarian, a therapist, and a writer. Her life had great troubles: her beloved daughter Lucy died when she was only seven, and her son Ian has fought illness all his life. She also knew great joy with a love and a marriage that caught her by surprise late in her life. She wound her long, eventful life into stories.

Joan believed passionately that stories have a power we can barely understand. They can heal us, comfort us, propel us to greatness. Thousands of people have listened to Joan, often in the most unlikely of places. She could be found telling the tales at street corners, coffee shops, by hospital beds, and on any kind of transport you can name. Imagine telling "Burd Janet" aboard a 747. She did it.

This is Joan's last children's book. Now the stories are yours. Read them. Better yet, tell them in your own voice so that you too take your place, linked to the storytellers whose voices still echo in these stories as they did in the great halls so long ago.

YOUNG TRISTAN

ong ago, when King Mark ruled over Cornwall, King Rivalen of Lyonesse heard that Mark's enemies made war on him, so he sailed across the sea to aid his ally. So well did Rivalen serve him, with counsel and with sword, that Mark gave to him his thirteen-year-old sister, Blanchefleur, whom Rivalen did love marvelously. When Rivalen asked her to marry him, plighted his troth, he gave to her a gold ring, set with pearls and rubies.

They were married by Saint Sampson in the chapel at Golant, scarce a mile over the fields from Mark's castle. Shortly after their wedding night, news came that Rivalen's old enemy, Duke Morgan, had landed in Lyonesse, seeking land and kingship. Summoning his barons, the rightful king sailed back to his own country, taking Blanchefleur with him, although she was with

child. She was with child! They landed at the fortress of
Highknoll, where Rivalen's people rallied. Rivalen left
Blanchefleur in the care of his grizzled steward, Rohalt,
then went off to wage his war. His war!

Blanchefleur waited for Rivalen, she waited weeks
and months most patiently, until word finally came
that her husband had been killed in an ambush most
foul. She did not weep. She gave no cry or lamenta-
tion, but turned her face to the wall. Gruff old Rohalt
tried to comfort her. "Lady," he said, "do not pile grief
on grief. Better it is to praise life and living than to
pine for the dead."

She gave no sign that she had heard him. Her limbs
wasted and she barely ate or drank; if so, only for the
sake of her unborn child. After the birth, Blanchefleur
took her baby in her arms and said, "Little son, I have
waited a long time for you. Now that I hold you, I see
the fairest thing a woman ever saw. In sorrow did I come
here. In sorrow did I bring you forth. In sorrow has your
first feast day come and gone. So I shall call you Tristan,
which is another name for sorrow." Having said these
words, she kissed him – and having kissed him, she died.

Now Rohalt's duty was to the baby's preservation.
Even as he feigned allegiance to Duke Morgan, he hid
Rivalen and Blanchefleur's son in his own household,
among his legal children and grandchildren. When

seven years had passed, and it was time to take him from
the women, Rohalt gave Tristan over to the care of a
wise tutor, the squire Gorvenal. In the next few years,
Gorvenal taught Tristan everything a knight should
know: how to use sword and escutcheon, arrow, spear
and lance, and how to throw stone quoits unerringly. He
trained him to wrestle and to swim, to run fast for short
distances, and to endure for long, to leap wide ditches,
to climb high walls, and to scramble over banks and
mounds. And oh, if you could have seen the lad as he
rode among the young squires, broad in the shoulders
and strong in the thighs, so determined, loyal, and full
of grace, you would have thought that he and his horse
and his armor were all one being.

In addition, Gorvenal taught Tristan to keep his word,
and to hate every lie and felony. And, noticing the boy's
special promise, which he knew he could not alone
fulfill, the squire persuaded Rohalt to send for a master
from Brittany, who taught the lad how to play the harp,
and schooled him in song and story. But the most pow-
erful learning imparted to Tristan was by Gorvenal
himself: not only the skill of hunting, but the art; not
only the art, but the mystery. He initiated Tristan into
the secrets of life and death by teaching the young
acolyte how to show respect for the animal he had
killed, and to atone for that killing by certain rites and

rituals. All the world complimented Rohalt for having such a son. And Rohalt, loving Tristan as a son, yet revered him as his lord and king, for he knew that all that grace and strength was the result of the union of Rivalen of Lyonesse and of Blanchefleur, sister to the king of Cornwall. Tristan was their resurrection.

But all Rohalt's joy was snatched away on the day when certain merchants of Norway stole Tristan as a rich prize (though the boy fought hard, like a young wolf caught in a trap). Hardly had the Norwegians' ship cleared port than the sea rose and cast an angry storm round it. For eight days and eight nights, they were driven at random; then, through the mists, the sailors caught a glimpse of awful cliffs and seaward rocks. The sea would have ground their hull to pieces thereon, but just in the nick o' time they thought to give penance, for they knew the storm came of the lad whom they had stolen, on evil impulse, by luring him aboard their vessel. The whole crew went to the captain to plead for Tristan's deliverance; he vowed he would lower the Jonah overside, in a small boat. Then wind and sea fell, and the sky shone. As the Norwegian ship grew tiny in the offing, a returning tide cast Tristan, in his boat, upon a beach of sand.

Painfully he climbed the cliff and saw a bracken-covered heath, studded with boulders, and a circle of

stones, man hewn, for which he set out. Beyond the
heath a forest stretched, dark and endless. Tristan
wept! He wept for his tutor, Gorvenal, and for Rohalt,
whom he thought to be his father. He wept for the
land of Lyonesse.

Just as he gained the shelter of the circle, he heard
the sound of a hunt, and a tall stag broke cover at the
forest's edge. Pack and hunt streamed after it, with a
tumult of cries and a sounding of horns. As the hounds
were racing, clustered at the haunch, the stag turned at
bay, not a stone's throw from Tristan. The chief huntsman rushed forward and gave the final thrust, while all
around the hunt was gathering, with yelp and babble
and winding of horns.

But Tristan, when he saw the huntsman take up a
knife and make as though he would hack off the head of
the stag, remembered the teachings of Gorvenal. He
could contain himself no longer. Although he was
weaponless, and a castaway lad in a strange land, he
nevertheless stepped out from among the stones to
protest the blasphemy. "My lord, what are you doing?
Are you going to cut up so noble a beast, like any farm-
yard hog? Is that the custom of this country?"

And the huntsman answered, "Fair stranger, what's
the problem? Why yes, first I take off the head of the
stag, then I cut it into quarters, and four of us carry the

pieces home on our saddle-bows, to our master, the King of Cornwall. That's what we do and that's what we've always done, as far back as I know, although I have heard tales that make me wonder. If you know of some better custom, then teach it to us. Here, take this knife. Gladly will we watch you."

Tristan knelt and showed the hunters how to skin the stag before he dismembered it. As he worked he put aside the head, the haunch, the tongue, and the great heart's vein. The huntsmen and the kennel men stood over him, delighting in his skill, and gasped with wonder when he removed the crowbone and threw it skyward. The birds of the air swooped down to grasp it, so as to carry it Heavenward. All this in honor of the animal they had just killed!

The master huntsmen said, "Friend, these are good ways. Where did you learn them? What country do you come from, and what is your name?"

"Good lord, my name is Tristan, and I come from the country of Lyonesse. I was taught these ways by a man wise in the invocation of ancient powers."

"Tristan," mused the master huntsman, "God reward the father who brought you up so well. No doubt he is a baron, rich and strong?"

Now Tristan had learned a thing or three while he

was aboard the Norwegian ship. Warily, he answered, "Why no, my lord. My father is a free man, a mere burgess. We had a quarrel, which I now regret, and I ran away to sea. I wished to know how men live in foreign lands, but the ship on which I traveled was wrecked during a storm. I was barely able to climb aboard an empty shallop and so float to your shore. But if you will accept me of this hunt, I will follow you gladly and teach you other crafts and rituals."

"Tristan, I marvel that in your land a burgess's son knows more than a knight's son knows here in Cornwall. Come with us, since you will it, and we will take you to our lord. But first, show us more of your art."

Tristan completed his task, explaining all the while as he taught the huntsmen how the ordering should be done. To the one he gave the right antler, and to another the left antler. Then he instructed the kennel men how to thread the pieces on pikes and gave to one hunter the snout, to others a haunch, to others a flank, to others the chine, and he taught them to arrange themselves, two by two, in order, each according to the dignity of his piece. Then he showed four huntsmen how to make a canopy, tying each corner of the hide to a pike, and that canopy was held high over the procession. As they moved through the forest, the kennel men dancing to the beat of a drum, and the huntsmen's horses almost dancing too, the stag that had been so noble in life was made larger and holier in death.

So they took the road and spoke together, till they came upon a castle made of great stones, like a chessboard of green and blue. All around it were orchards and plow lands, and fields and fish ponds and living waters. Well fenced against assault and engines of war, the castle stood above the sea and looked down upon an estuary and the port of Foy. Many ships were in the harbor.

"What name do you give this castle?" asked Tristan.

"Fair liege," they said, "we call it Castle Dore."

"Castle Dore! Blessed be thou of God, and blessed be they that dwell within thee." (Therein, my lords and ladies, therein had his father, the king of Lyonesse, taken his mother, a princess of Cornwall, to wife, though their son knew it not.)

When they came up to the keep, the horns brought the baron – and King Mark, himself – to the gate. The master huntsman told his story, and King Mark marveled at the high art of venery, and how the stag was honored and elevated by great skill and ceremony. Most he marveled at the young stranger and gazed at him tenderly yet troubled, wondering whence came his tenderness. His heart answered him nothing, but it was blood that spoke, my lords and ladies. Blood! And the love he bore his long-lost sister, Blanchefleur.

That evening when the boards were cleared, a singer out of Wales, a master, came forward with his harp and sang of the loves of Graelant. As his fingers left the strings, Tristan, who sat at the king's feet, spoke to him. "Oh master, that ancient song from Breton is seldom heard nowadays. Few know the words, and fewer still the tune. Your choice is subtle, master. You harp us well."

"Boy," spake the bard, "how come you to know so much about music? Do mere burgesses from Lyonesse have their sons taught harp play, and rote and viol too? If so, take you this harp and show us what you can do."

Then Tristan took the harp and sang so well that the barons' hearts were softened. King Mark, listening to the castaway from Lyonesse, bethought himself of that land, and mourned again for Blanchefleur, who, it was rumored, had died in childbirth; and for his friend and ally, Rivalen, killed in an ambush. Had he sinned, to let his little sister go to such a far and dangerous place?

When the song ended, the king sat silent for a long space. Then he spoke, "Blessed be the master who taught thee, and blessed be thou of God, for God loves good singers and storytellers. Their voices and the voice of the harp wake dear memories, and salve us of many a grief and many a sin. For our joy did you come to this roof, friend. Stay near us a long time."

As the court watched, Tristan kneeled before the king. Strong and clear his voice rang out, "Very willingly will I serve you, sire, as your harper, and your huntsman, and your liege."

So he did for three years. By day, Tristan followed King Mark as he rode about his kingdom, listening to pleas, talking with his vassals, inspecting troops and battlements. By night, Tristan slept in the royal bedchamber with the councillors and the peers. If the king was sad or troubled, Tristan would play the harp to soothe his care; if the king would merry be, his harper matched his mood. The barons cherished him, but more tenderly than the barons, the king loved him. Yet Tristan could not forget Rohalt, his father, nor Gorvenal, his teacher.

My lords and ladies, a teller who would please should not stretch his tale too long. In a nutshell, then, when three years had passed and Tristan had grown to be almost a man, Rohalt arrived in Cornwall with his squire, Gorvenal, after long wandering by sea and land. When he came into the presence of King Mark's court, he espied Tristan immediately and they fell into each other's arms. Then producing a gold ring set with pearls and rubies, Gorvenal showed it to King Mark, who recognized it as the ring given by Rivalen to his sister, Blanchefleur.

Rohalt announced before all the court, "King Mark, here is your nephew Tristan, son of your sister, Blanchefleur, and King Rivalen of Lyonesse. Duke Morgan holds his land most wrongfully. It is time the rightful heir take it back again."

On hearing this, King Mark dubbed his nephew and armed him as a knight. Tristan, with Rohalt and Gorvenal, crossed the sea, rallied his vassals around him, and challenged Duke Morgan to battle. When Tristan had killed his true father's slayer and was reseized of his land, he called his barons to assemble and said, "My lords, God the Father watches over me always, and so have three other fathers. Rohalt, my father's steward, took me as an orphan babe and hid me, at great risk, with his own children. Gorvenal, my teacher, treated me as though I were his own son. And King Mark, my mother's brother, has shown familial love for me these past three years, even though he knew not that I was of his own blood.

"Now a free man has two things thoroughly his own: his land and his body. To Rohalt and all the sons who follow him, I here and now release my land and kingdom, but my body I will give up to King Mark. Already I have pledged to be his harper and his huntsman and his liege.

I will leave this country, dear that it be. I will betake myself to Cornwall, where I will serve King Mark as my lord. Such is my decision.

"You, my lords of Lyonesse, are my lieges, and therefore owe me counsel. If any one of you would counsel me another way, let him rise and speak now." The barons wept to hear him, even as they praised him for choosing Rohalt to be their king. Not one of the barons said him nay. Then, taking Gorvenal only with him, Tristan set sail for King Mark's land.

TO THE DARK TOWER

Childe Rowland and his brothers twain
Were playing at the ball,
And there was their sister,
The beautiful Burd Ellen,
In the midst, among them all.

Childe Rowland kicked it with his foot
And caught it with his knee;
At last, as he plunged among them all
O'er the church he made it flee.

Burd Ellen round about the aisle
To seek the ball is gone,
But long they waited and longer still,
And she came not back again.

They sought her east, they sought her west,
They sought her up and down,
And woe were the hearts of those brethren,

For she was not to be found.

o her eldest brothers went to the Warlock Merlin and told him all that had happened, and asked him if he knew where Burd Ellen was. "The fair Burd Ellen," quavered Merlin, "must have been carried off by the elves, because she went round the church widershins – the opposite way to the sun. She is now in the Dark Tower of the King of Elfland. It would take the boldest knight in the world to bring her back."

"If it is possible to bring her back," said her brother, "We'll do it or perish in the attempt."

"Possible, it is," said Merlin, "but woe to the man or mother's son that attempts it, if he is not well taught beforehand what he is to do."

The eldest brothers of Burd Ellen were not to be put off, by any fear of danger, from attempting to get her back, so they begged the Warlock Merlin to tell them what they should do, and what they should not do, in seeking out their sister. And after they had been taught and had repeated their lesson, they set out for Elfland, to the Dark Tower.

But long they waited, and longer still,
With doubt and muckle pain,
But woe were the hearts of their brethren,

For they came not back again.

And when they had waited and waited and waited a good long time, the youngest of Burd Ellen's brothers, Childe Rowland, wished to go. He went to his mother to ask her permission. But she would not allow him at first, for he was the last and dearest of her children, and if he was lost, all would be lost. But he begged and he begged, till she finally gave her blessing, and also gave him his father's good brand that never struck in vain. As she buckled it round his waist, she wove a weird into the steel, patterned with dragons and twisting tendrils, and she chanted the victory spell.

So Childe Rowland said good-bye to his mother, and set out for the cave of the Warlock Merlin. "Once more, and but once more," he said to Merlin, "tell how man or mother's son may rescue my sister and my brothers."

"Well, my son," said Merlin, "there is one thing to do, over and over, and two things not to do: sip not a sip and bite not a bit all the time thou art in the Elfland, no matter how hungry or thirsty thou art."

"And the thing that I must do?" asked Childe Rowland.

"Once you enter into the land of the elves," said Merlin, "you must out, with your father's good brand that never struck in vain, and cut off the head of whomever you meet – except, of course, until you meet your sister, the beautiful Burd Ellen. Do and not do as I have told thee, or else you will never see Middle Earth again."

So Childe Rowland said these things over and over again, till he knew them by heart, and he thanked the Warlock Merlin and went on his way. And he went along and along and along, and still farther along, till he came to a herd of feeding horses that had fiery eyes and struck up fire from their hooves, which meant that he was at last in Elfland. "Can you tell me," asked Childe Rowland of the horseherd, "where the King of Elfland's Dark Tower is?"

"How should I know?" answered the horseherd, scratching his chin. "Go along the road and ask the cowherd." With knightly courtesy, Childe Rowland thanked him, then pulled out the good brand that never struck in vain and – swish-swash-swoosh – off went the horseherd's head! Childe Rowland went along farther, and a little farther, till he came to the cowherd. "Can you tell me where the King of Elfland's Dark Tower is?"

"I dunno," said the cowherd, scratching his head. "Why're you asking me? Go down the road to the hen-wife. She knows everything." Childe Rowland thanked him too, then drew out the good brand that never struck in vain and – swish-swash-swoosh – off went the cowherd's head!

He went a little farther, till he came to an old woman in a gray cloak. She was feeding the ducks and chickens clustered around her skirt, and he asked her if she knew where the Dark Tower of the King of Elfland was. "Aye, that I do," said she. "Go down this road apiece and you will come to a round green hill, all ringed about with terraces, from the bottom to the top. Circle it three times widershins, and each time say, 'Open, door! Open, door! Let me come in,' and the third time the door will open, and you may go in."

Childe Rowland thanked her politely and then set off again: one foot, then the other; one foot, then the other, one foot, then . . . But, oh! What had he forgotten? Yes! Back he went with long quick strides, out came the good brand that never struck in vain and – swish-swash-swoosh – off went the hen-wife's head!

At last he came to the round green hill with the terrace-rings from top to bottom, and he circled it three times widershins, saying each time, "Open, door! Open, door! Let me come in." The third time the door did open, and Childe Rowland stepped over the threshold. The door closed behind him with a click.

Childe Rowland had entered the Dark Tower.

Close your eyes! You may think you know how dark it was in there, but it was darker still. After a while, Childe Rowland was able to see a dim glow, a sort of twilight or gloaming, and a corridor stretching before him. There were neither windows nor torches, and he could not make out where the twilight came from, if not through the walls and roof. Rough arches, made of transparent rock, were encrusted with sheepsilver and rockspar and other shiny stones. But though all was rock, the air was quite warm, as it always is in Elfland. Wondering as he went, Childe Rowland continued along the passage until he came to two wide and high doors, almost as big as the doors of a cathedral. He slipped through the space between them to enter a large and spacious hall, almost as large as the green hill itself. The roof was supported by fine pillars, so thick and lofty that the pillars of a cathedral were as nothing to them. They were all of gold and silver, with fretted work, and between them and around them wreaths of flowers, composed of what, do you think? Why, of diamonds and emeralds, and all manner of precious stones. And the very key-stones of the arches had for ornaments clusters of pearls, with rubies and other jewels. And all these arches met in the middle of the roof, and just there, hung by a gold chain, was an immense lamp made out of one big, hollowed-out, transparent pearl. And in the middle of this was a huge ruby, which kept spinning round and round, running shivers of crimson up and down the walls and lighting the whole hall, as if the setting sun was shining on it.

The hall was furnished in a manner equally grand, and at one end of it on a glorious couch of velvet, silk, and gold sat Burd Ellen, combing her blond hair with a silver comb. And when she saw Childe Rowland, she stood up and they rushed into each other's arms. Then she said:

"God pity ye, poor luckless fool,
What have ye here to do?

"Hear ye this, my youngest brother,
Why didn't ye bide at home?
Had you a hundred thousand lives
Ye couldn't spare any a one.

"But sit ye down; but woe, O, woe,
That ever ye were born,
For come the King of Elfland in,

Your fortune is forlorn."

Then they sat down together, and Childe Rowland told her all that he had done, and she told him how their two brothers had reached the Dark Tower but had been enchanted by the King of Elfland and lay nearby in another room, as though entombed and dead.

Childe Rowland was beginning to feel weak after his long travels, so he asked his sister for food and drink. What had he forgotten? Why, the Warlock Merlin's warning, of course: "Sip not a sip and bite not a bit, all the time thou art in Elfland." Burd Ellen looked at her brother sadly, but she was under a spell and could not remind him. So she rose up and left, and soon brought back a silver basin, chased all round with horned gods and scenes of the hunt; it was full of a posset of bread and milk. Childe Rowland was just about to raise it to his lips when he looked at his sister and remembered why he had come all this way. He dashed the bowl to the ground, saying, "Not a sip will I sip, not a bit will I bite, till Burd Ellen is set free."

At that moment they heard the noise of someone approaching and a loud voice shouting:

> "Fee, fi, fo, fum,
> I smell the blood of an English man;
> Be he alive or be he dead,

I'll dash his brains from his brain-pan."

And then the doors of the hall burst open, and the King of Elfland charged in.

"Strike then, Bogle, if you dare," shouted Childe Rowland, and rushed to meet him with his father's good brand that never yet did fail. They fought and they fought and they fought, till Childe Rowland beat the king down on his knees and caused him to beg for mercy.

"I'll grant you mercy when you release my sister from your spells and raise my brothers to life and let us all go free," said Childe Rowland. "Then, and only then, shall you be spared."

"I agree, I agree," growled the king. Rising up, he went to a chest from which he took a small glass jar filled with a blood-red liquid. With this he anointed the ears, eyelids, nostrils, lips, and fingertips of the two brothers, and they sprang at once into life, and declared that their souls had been away but had now returned.

Then, with Childe Rowland pricking at his throat, the Elf King muttered some words over Burd Ellen, and she was disenchanted. They all four went out through the hall, through the great doors, down the long passage, and back to Middle Earth. Forever after, neither

Childe Rowland, nor his sister, Burd Ellen, nor his brothers twain, nor their noble mother, ever went around a church widershins again.

IRON JOHN

nce upon a time there was a great forest, filled with wild animals and things so mysterious that no man could name. At the edge of the forest there was a castle, where lived a wealthy king. He viewed the forest as his private preserve, as his father had before him. One day he sent out a huntsman to shoot him a roe, but the huntsman did not come back. "Perhaps some accident has befallen him," said the king. The next day, he sent out two huntsmen to search for the first, but they, too, did not return. On the third day, he sent for all his huntsmen and said, "Scour the whole forest through, and do not give up until you have found all three." But of these also, none came home again, and as for the pack of hounds, not one of them was ever seen more. From that time forth, no one would venture into the forest, and it lay in such deep stillness and solitude that if the greatest oak in the kingdom had fallen, there would have been no one to hear it, nor vouch for its falling. Once in a while a hawk or an eagle was seen to fly over the tree-tops, but what may have been thus witnessed from the air remained a secret, and only added to the mystery of the abandoned woods.

Years passed, then one day a stranger came to court and presented himself to the king. He was a huntsman seeking employment. To prove his worth, he offered to go into the dangerous forest. The king, who was not only prudent but kind, would not give his consent. He said, "It's not safe in there. I fear it would fare with you no better than with the others, and you would never come out again."

"Lord," said the huntsman, "I will take responsibility for my own risk." And so saying, he whistled for his hound dog and set out on an overgrown path into the forest. No sooner had he entered among the trees' deep shadow than his hound fell in with sign and scent of game and loped off in pursuit. When the huntsman caught up, he found his dog standing before a great pool. And while he watched, a naked arm stretched out of the water, seized the dog, and drew it under. Determined to save his hound, he returned to the castle to fetch hewers and drawers to drain the pool with their buckets. When they could see to the bottom, there was no sign of the dog, but there lay a wild man whose body was brown like rusty iron, and whose hair hung over his face down to his knees. They bound the man with chains and led him away. Back at the palace, there was great astonishment at the wild man. The king had him put in an iron cage in his courtyard and forbade the door to be opened, on pain of death. And the queen took the key into her own keeping.

The king and queen had an eight-year-old son who often played in the courtyard. One day, his golden ball rolled into the cage. The boy ran up to the cage and said to the wild man, "Give me my ball."

"Not till thou opens the cage for me," replied the wild man.

"No, I will not do that," said the boy. "My father has forbidden it," and he ran away. The next day he again asked for his ball. The wild man said, "Open the cage door," but the boy would not. On the following day, the king and all his court went hunting. The boy returned to the cage once more and said, "I can't open the door, even if I wanted to. I don't have the key. It's under my mother's pillow."

"Sooner or later," said the wild man, "every boy must steal the key from under his mother's pillow." The boy, who yearned for his golden ball, cast all thought to the winds. He mounted the tower stairs, crept into his mother's bedchamber, slid his hand under her pillow, and stole the key. But when he tried to open the cage door, he found that the task was not an easy one; he pinched his finger on a rusty hinge. However, the cage opened, and the wild man stepped out. Keeping his part of the bargain, he handed the ball to the boy before he hurried away. But the boy had become afraid; he called and cried after him, "Oh wild man, please don't leave me. I shall be beaten, or even worse!" The wild man turned back, took the royal boy on his shoulder, and strode with hasty steps into the forest.

When the king returned, he saw the empty cage in the courtyard and asked the queen what had happened. She knew nothing about it and sought the key, but it was gone. She called the boy, but he did not answer. Servants searched the entire castle, from tower to dungeon, from throne room to scullery, but the boy was not anywhere. The king sent out people to seek for him in the fields and copses, but they did not find him. He could easily guess what had happened. He and the queen fell into each other's arms, weeping, and grief reigned throughout the royal court.

When the wild man had reached the deepest, darkest part of the forest, he took the boy down from his shoulders and said, "Thou will never see thy father or mother again, but don't worry. I will keep thee here with me, for thou art the one who set me free; besides, I have taken a liking to thee. Henceforth thou will call me by my name, which is Iron John. If thou dost what I tell thee to do, thou will fare well. Of treasure and gold I have not only enough, but more than anyone else in the world." He made a bed of moss, on which the boy lay himself down to sleep.

The next morning, Iron John took the boy to a well-spring in the forest and said, "Behold, this spring is bright and clear as crystal. Thy charge is to sit beside it and to see that nothing touches it, or falls into it, or else it will be polluted. I will come every evening to see if thou hast obeyed my order." The boy sat on the curb that edged the well, and often he saw a golden fish or a golden snake flick past in the depths, and he took care that nothing should fall in or touch the water. As the day wore on, his injured finger hurt him so violently that he involuntarily put it into the water. He drew it quickly out again, but the harm was done. His finger was covered with gold, and try as he might he could not rub off the gilding. His finger sparkled in those few motes and beams of sunlight that penetrated to the forest floor.

In the evening, Iron John came back, looked at the boy, and said, "What has happened to the well?"

"Nothing happened," said the boy and held his finger behind his back, hoping that the wild man would not see it. But Iron John said, "Thou hast dipped thy finger into the water. This time I shall let it pass, but take care that nothing else goes in." By daybreak the boy was already sitting by the well and watching it. His finger hurt him again; to keep himself from making the same mistake twice he buried it in his long, thick hair. Unhappily, a hair fell down into the well. He hooked his golden finger and took it quickly out, but alas, it was gilded! When Iron John came in the evening, he already knew what had happened. "Thou hast let a hair fall into my well," he said. "I will let thee watch by it one more time, but I warn thee that if it happens for the third time, that the well is polluted, thou can no longer remain with me."

On the third day, the boy sat by the well and did not so much as twitch his finger, no matter how much it hurt. But the time was long to him; he entertained himself by making faces at himself, reflected on the water's surface. But even of that pastime he wearied. His head nodded, and as he bent down more and more, trying to keep himself awake by looking straight into his eyes, his long hair flipped over the crown of his head and the loose strands trailed into the water. Instantly, his entire hair was gilded from ends to roots. His head

shone like the sun. The boy was terrified, and fished in
his pocket to find a kerchief. He tied it around his head,
but when Iron John came in the evening he already
knew what had happened and said, "Take off thy kerchief." Then the golden hair streamed forth, and no
excuses would avail. "Thou has not stood the trial," said
Iron John, "and cannot stay here with me. Go into the
world, and there learn what poverty is. But as thou dost
not have a bad heart, and as I mean well by thee, there
is one thing I will grant thee: if thou fallest into great
difficulty, come to the forest and cry, 'Iron John,' and I
will come and help thee. My power is great, greater than
thou thinkest, and I have gold and silver in abundance."

Then the king's son left the forest, and walked by
beaten and unbeaten paths ever onward until at length
he reached a great city. There he looked for work, but
could find none, for he had learned nothing by which
he could help himself, or anybody else for that matter.
He went to the castle and asked if they would take him
in. The court did not at all know what use to make of
him, but the boy was likable and mannerly, and they
allowed him to stay around. The cook said that he
might carry food and water, and rake the cinders. Once,
when it so happened that no one else was at hand, the
cook ordered him to carry the food to the royal table,

but as he did not like to let his golden hair be seen, he kept his kerchief on.

Such a custom as that had never come under the king's notice, and he said, "When you come to the royal table, you must take your kerchief off." The boy answered, "I am sorry, Lord, but I cannot. I have a bad sore on my head." Then the king had the cook called before him and scolded him, and asked how he could take such a boy as that into his service, and that he was to turn him out at once. The cook, however, had pity on him, and exchanged him for the gardener's son.

Now the boy had to plant and water the garden, hoe and dig, and bear the wind and bad weather. Once in summer, when he was working alone in the garden, he took his kerchief off so the air might cool him. As the sun shone on his hair, it glittered and flashed so that the rays fell into the bower of the king's daughter, and up she sprang to see what it could be. Then she saw the boy and cried to him, "Boy, bring me a wreath of flowers." He capped his head with all haste, went into the fields, and gathered bunches of wildflowers, which he bound and wove together. When he was ascending the stairs with them, the gardener met him and said, "How can you take the king's daughter a garland of such common flowers? Go back into the gardens and pick for her only those kinds that are rare and cultivated."

"She prefers the wild ones," said the boy. And he continued to ascend the stairs.

When he got into the room, the king's daughter said, "Take your kerchief off, it is not seemly to remain capped in my presence." He again said, "I may not. I have a sore on my head." She, however caught at his kerchief and pulled it off, and then his golden hair rolled down on his shoulders and it was splendid to behold. He tried to run out, but she grabbed him by the arm and gave him a handful of ducats. With these he departed, but he cared nothing for the golden pieces. He took them to the gardener and said, "Give them to your children. They can play with them."

The following day, the king's daughter again called to him that he was to bring her a wreath – and to make sure they were field flowers. When he arrived with the wreath, she instantly snatched at his kerchief to take it away from him, but he held it fast with both hands. She again gave him a handful of ducats, but he again gave them to the gardener's children. On the third day, things went just the same; she could not get his kerchief away from him, and he gave away the money.

Not long afterward, the country was overrun by war. The king gathered together his people, but he did not know whether he could offer enough opposition to the enemy, which was superior in strength and had a mighty army. The gardener's boy offered, "I am grown up enough to go to war. Give me a horse!" The others laughed and said, "Seek one for yourself when we are gone. We will leave one in the stable for you." When they had gone forth, he went into the stable for the horse. It was lame in one foot and limped, hobblety-jig, hobblety-jig. Nevertheless, the boy mounted it and rode away, not toward the battlefield, but toward the dark and mysterious forest. When he came to the edge, he called, "Iron John! Iron John! Iron John!" so loudly that the name echoed through the trees. Thereupon the wild man appeared.

"What dost thou desire?" he asked.

"I want a strong steed, for I am going to the war."

"That thou shalt have, and still more than thou askest for." Then Iron John went back into the forest, but it was not long before a stableman came out from among the trees, leading a horse that snorted and pranced and could hardly be restrained. And behind them followed a great troop of soldiers, entirely equipped in iron, and their swords flashed in the sun. The youth made over his lame horse to the hostler, mounted the spirited steed, and rode at the head of the iron-clad troop. By the time he got near the battlefield, a great part of the king's men had already fallen, and little was wanting to make the rest run away. Then the youth galloped hither and yon with his iron soldiers, broke like a hurricane over the enemy. The other side fled, but the youth rallied his own and the king's army to pursue, and didn't stop until every one of the opponents was either dead or taken prisoner. Instead of returning to the king, however, he conducted the troop by back roads and lonely tracks that led to the forest. "Iron John! Iron John! Iron John!" he cried.

"What dost thou desire?"

"Take back your horse and your iron troop, and give me my hobblety nag again." All that he asked was done, and soon he was riding, hobblety-jig, hobblety-jig, back to the castle.

Meanwhile, the king had returned. His daughter was waiting for him by the drawbridge gate, to wish him great joy of his victory. "I am not the one who carried the day," he said. "We owe our survival to a strange knight who came to my aid with his soldiers when things looked their worst." His daughter wanted to hear who the strange knight was, but the king did not know and said, "He rode off to the edge of the battlefield and disappeared in the dust and mist. Neither I nor anyone else did see him again." The princess went down into the gardens and inquired of the gardener where his boy was, but he smiled and said, "He has just come home on his jaded nag, and the others have been mocking him and crying, 'Here comes our hobblety-jig home again!' They asked too, 'Under what hedge have you been sleeping all this time?' You will hardly believe, ma'am, that cheeky boy's reply: 'I did the best of all, and it would have gone badly without me.' And then he was still more ridiculed. And rightly so!"

The princess prevailed upon her father to proclaim a great feast in celebration of the victory. The feast would last for three days. "Father, you must announce that I shall throw a golden apple and that I will make my champion whoever catches it for three days running. Perhaps the unknown knight will attend as a courtesy to you, and you will be able to thank him." When the feast was announced, the youth went into the forest and called for Iron John.

"What dost thou desire?" asked he.

"That I may catch the king's daughter's golden apple."

"It is as safe as if thou hadst it already. Thou shalt likewise have a suit of bronze armor for the occasion, and ride a roan-colored horse."

When the day came, the youth galloped to the spot, took his place among the knights, and was recognized by no one. The king's daughter came forward and threw a golden apple to the knights, but none of them caught

it but he. As soon as he had it, he galloped away. On the
second day, Iron John equipped him with armor of
silvery steel and gave him a white horse. Again he was
the only one who caught the apple, but he did not
linger an instant, and galloped off with it. The king
grew angry and said, "That is not allowed. He must
appear before me and give me his name, else I deem him
churlish." He gave the order that if the knight that
caught the apple should go away again, they should
pursue him, and if he did not come back willingly, they
were to cut him down and stab him.

On the third day, he received from Iron John a suit of
black armor and a black horse, and again he caught the
apple. But when he was riding off with it, the king's
attendants pursued him, and one of them got so near
him that he wounded the youth's leg with the point of
his sword. The youth nevertheless escaped from them,
but his horse leapt so violently that his helmet fell off,
and then they saw his head was covered with glittering
gold, and that golden hair streamed out behind him.
They rode back and announced the marvel to the king.

The following day, the king's daughter asked the gardener about his boy. "He is at work now in the garden, as
he should be, but the queer creature has been sneaking
off to the festival. Last night, when he came home, he
gave my children three gold-colored apples, which he said

he had won fairly. Some months ago he gave them false ducats to play with. Of course I know the gold is not real, but the children delight in them even so."

The king had the gardener's boy summoned to court. He came, with the kerchief on his head. But the king's daughter went up to him and snatched it off. Then his golden hair fell down over his shoulders, and he was so handsome that all were amazed. "Are you the knight who came every day to the festival, always in different colors, and who caught the three golden apples?" asked the king.

"Yes," answered the youth, "and here the apples are," and he took them out of his pocket and returned them to the king. "If you want further proof, you may see the wound your people gave me when they followed me. But I am likewise the knight who helped you to victory over your enemies."

"If you can perform such deeds as that, you are no ordinary gardener's boy. Tell me, who is your father?" asked the king.

"My father is a mighty king, who lives on the other side of the forest."

"I well see," said the king, "that I owe thanks to you. Can I do anything to please you?"

"Yes," answered the youth, "as a matter of fact you can. Give me your daughter to wife."

The maiden laughed and said, "He does not stand
much on ceremony, but I have already seen that he is no
gardener's boy – and not just because of his golden hair."
And then she kissed him.

Word was sent out throughout the kingdom, and to
all the kingdoms around, that the king's daughter was to
marry a prince. His father and mother came to the
wedding, and were in great delight, for they had given
up hope of ever seeing their dear son again. And as they
were sitting at the marriage feast, the music suddenly
stopped, the doors opened, and a king more stately than
any other came in with a great entourage. He went up
to the youth, embraced him, and said:

"I am Iron John, and it was by enchantment that I
was held at the bottom of the pool, then in a cage,
where I was made a mere showpiece, and was rusting
away. But when thou stolest the key from underneath
thy mother's pillow, thou set me free to live in the
greenwood again, which is my natural dominion and
storehouse, held for the common good. All treasures
and mysteries that I possess shall be thine, for thou art
my true heir."

And from that time onward, everyone could roam
safely throughout the forest.

BURD JANET

oung Tamlane was son of Earl Murray, and
Burd Janet was daughter of Dunbar, Earl of
March. When they were young, they loved
each other and promised to marry, but when the time
came near for their wedding, Tamlane disappeared, and
none knew what had become of him.

Many days after he had disappeared, Burd Janet was
wandering in Caterhaugh Wood, a dark and dangerous
place where her old nurse had warned her never to go.
As she wandered, she plucked flowers from the bushes.
She came at last to a green mound, where grew a bush of
broom, and began to pick the yellow blossoms. She had
not taken more than three flowerets when by her side
appeared young Tamlane.

"Where come ye from, Tamlane?" asked Burd Janet.
"And why have you been away so long?"

"From Elfland I come," answered young Tamlane. "The Queen of Elfland has made me her knight."

"But how did you get there?" said Burd Janet.

"I was a-hunting one day, and as I rode widershins around yon green mound, a deep drowsiness fell upon me. When I awoke, behold! I was in Elfland. Fair is that land, and merry too, and fain would I stop there but for thee. And one other thing."

"Pray tell me, Tamlane, what is that thing?"

"Every seven years the elves pay their tithe to the netherworld, and for all the queen makes much of me, I fear it is myself will be that tithe."

"Oh, can you be saved? Tell me if aught I can do will save thee, Tamlane?"

"There is but one chance. Tomorrow night is Hallowe'en, the only time in the whole year when I might be snatched to my safety. On Hallowe'en night, the elfin court rides through England and Scotland, from Landsend to John-o-groats, in full panoply. If you would rescue me from Elfland, you must venture into Caterhaugh Wood and take your stand here, by this mound and by the well at Miles Cross, between twelve and one 'o the night. Bring with you a jar of holy water held tight in your hand, and sprinkle a sacred compass all around you."

"But how shall I know you, Tamlane," asked Burd Janet, "amid so many knights I've never seen before?"

"The first troop of elves that comes by, let 'em pass, let 'em pass. Do naught and say naught. The second, you must bow your head and curtsey, although you say naught. But the third that comes by is the queen's court, and at the head rides the queen, herself. By her side I shall ride, upon a milk-white steed, with a star in my crown; they deem me this honor as being a mortal knight. Watch my hands, Janet: the right one will be gloved, but the left one will be bare. By that token shall ye know me."

"But how to save you, Tamlane?" asked Burd Janet.

"You must spring upon me sudden, and pull so hard that I will fall to the ground within the holy ring. Then seize me quick, whatever change befall me, for they will exercise all their magic on me. Cling hold to me, cling tight, till they turn me into a red-hot iron sword; then cast me into the well, and I will be turned back into a mother-naked man. Throw your green cloak over me and I will be yours, and be of the world again."

So Burd Janet promised to do all this for Tamlane, and next night at midnight she took her stand by the well at Miles Cross and cast a compass of holy water around her.

As she stood there, alone in Caterhaugh Wood, she could hear the leaves rustling in the autumn wind, and somewhere the hoot of an owl. Soon the elfin procession came riding by. First over the mound was a troop of black steeds; she did naught and said naught. Then came another troop, on steeds of brown; she said naught, but she did do reverence, as Tamlane had taught her. But now came the court of Elfland, all on milk-white steeds. She saw the queen, and by her side a helmed knight with a star in his crown; his one hand was gloved and the other left bare. She knew this was her Tamlane, and springing forward she grabbed the bridle of the milk-white steed and pulled its rider from the saddle with such force that he fell within the ring of holy water. As soon as he had touched the ground, she let go the bridle and seized him in her arms.

"He's won, he's won amongst us all!" shrieked out the eldritch crew, and they approached the very edge of the circle to try their spells on young Tamlane.

> First they turned him in Janet's arms, like
>   frozen Ice,
> then into a huge flame of roaring Fire. Then,
>   again, the
> Fire vanished, and an Adder was skipping
>   through her arms.
> But still she held on!

And then they turned him into a huge Snake
   that reared up,
as if to bite her. And yet she held on!

Then they turned him into a pair of Doves,
   fluttering
between her breasts, struggling in her arms,
almost flying away. But still she held on!

Then they turned him into a Swan with a
   long, strong neck, that
thrust and thrust and thrust. But still she held
   on! Then,
at last, they changed Tamlane into a red hot
   Sword.

But all the eerie magic was in vain, for Burd Janet
plunged the fiery Sword into the well, and there she
was, holding naught but a mother-naked man in her
arms! Quickly she cast her green mantle over him, and
young Tamlane was Burd Janet's forever.

   Then the court turned away, to resume its march,
except for the queen. She paused and looked back,
then rode her horse to the very rim of the ring. There,
she sang:

"She that has borrowed young Tamlane
   Has gotten a stately groom,
She's taken away my bonniest knight,
   Left nothing in his room.

"But had I known, Tamlane, Tamlane,
   A lady would borrow thee,
I'd have taken out thy two gray eyes,
   Put in two eyne of tree.

"Had I but known, Tamlane, Tamlane,
   Before we came from home,
I'd have taken out thy heart of flesh,
   Put in a heart of stone.

"Had I but had the wit yestre'en
   That I have got today,
I'd have paid the Fiend seven times his teind
   Ere you'd been won away."

With a blast of wind and a rustle of leaves, the queen
and all her court rode off into the darkness. A great
silence followed, then Burd Janet took her husband's
hand, and together they ran home through Caterhaugh
Wood, back to her father's castle. There they were wel-
comed with a wedding feast.

THE WARRIOR QUEEN

ayve was Queen of Connaught, and Ahl-il was her husband. Their palace at Crooahnee was made of sweet-smelling cedar, painted and gilded. One night as they were lying in bed, their heads on a single pillow, they had this talk:

"It is true what they say, love," Ahl-il said. "It's well for the wife of a wealthy man."

"True enough," said Mayve. "But what made you say it?"

"Oh, it just occurred to me how much better off you are today than the day I married you."

"I was well enough off without you," said Mayve icily.

"Then your wealth was something I didn't hear much about," Ahl-il said. "Except for your woman's things. Maybe some talk when your raiding neighbors made off with a little loot and plunder."

"Not at all," she said. "But with the High King of Ireland for my father – Eocka Fidlic, the Steadfast? He, the son of Finn, the son of Finnoman, the son of Finnen? He, the son of Roth, the son of Regon, the son of Vlathackt, the son of Veothackt, the son of Enna Agneck, the son of Angus Turveck?

"And my father had six daughters: Dervroo, Ethna, Ella, Clothroo, Megan, and myself, Mayve, the highest and haughtiest. I outdid them all in grace and giving and battle and warlike combat. I had fifteen hundred soldiers in my royal pay, all exiles' sons, and the same number of freeborn native men, and for every paid soldier I had ten more men, and nine more, and eight and seven and six and five and four and three and two and one. And that was only our ordinary household.

"And my father – did I happen to mention he was the High King of Ireland? My father gave me a whole province of Ireland, and I rule that province from Crooahnee, which is why I am called 'Mayve of Crooahnee.' Royal messengers came, bearing messages their senders hoped would woo me. They came from Finn, the King of Leinster – Russ Ruahd's son. From Coipre Niafer, the King of Temair, another of Russ Ruahd's sons. They came from Conckovor, King of Ulster, son of Fahctna, and even from Eoxhed Vec. But I wouldn't go. For I asked a harder wedding gift than any woman ever asked before from any man in Ireland – the absence of meanness and jealousy and fear.

"If I married a mean man, our union would be wrong, because I am so full of grace and giving. It would be an insult if I were more generous than my husband, but not if the two of us were equal in this. If my husband was a timid man, our union would be just as wrong, because I thrive on all sorts of trouble. It is an insult for a wife to be more spirited than her husband. If I married a jealous man, that union would be wrong too: I never had a man yet, Ahl-lil, without another man waiting in his shadow.

"So I got the kind of man I wanted: yourself, Ahl-lil, Russ Ruahd's other son! You aren't greedy, you aren't jealous, and you are never fearful. When we were promised, I brought to you the best wedding gifts a bride could ever bring. I brought you apparel enough for a dozen men, and a chariot cunningly made of wicker and copper, worth thrice seven bondsmaids. I gave you red gold, the width of your face, and light gold, the weight of your left arm. So, if anyone causes you shame or upset or trouble, the right to compensation is mine, Ahl-lil," Mayve said. "For you're a kept man, Ahl-lil!"

"How can you think such a thing?" asked Ahl-lil. "Two kings are my brothers – Coipre in Temair, and Finn over Leinster. I let them rule because they are

older than I am, not because they are better in grace
and giving. As for you, I had never heard of a woman
ruling a province before, so I decided to come and take a
look. The kingship here is mine, not because I am
married to you, but because I am successor to my
mother, Mata Muiresc, King Magda's daughter. And I
thought to myself, who better to be my queen than you,
Mayve, the daughter of the High King of Ireland?"

"It still remains," Mayve said, "that my fortune is
greater than yours."

"You amaze me," Ahl-lil said. "No one has more property or jewels or precious things than I have, and I can
prove it."

Then the lowliest of their possessions were brought
out, to see who had more property and jewels and precious things: their buckets and tubs and iron pots, their
jugs and washpails, their vessels with handles and
vessels without handles. Then their finger rings,
bracelets, torques, and gold treasures. Cedar chests were
opened, and their cloth was displayed: purple, blue,
black, green, yellow and yellow brown, plain gray and
many colored; cloth checked and striped and speckled
and plaided.

Their herds of sheep were taken in off the fields and
meadows and plains. They were measured and matched
and found to be the same in numbers and size. Even the

great ram leading Mayve's sheep, the worth of one
bondsmaid by himself, had a ram to match him, leading
Ahl-lil's sheep. From pasture and paddock their teams
and herds of horses were brought in. For the finest stallion in Mayve's stud, also worth one bondsmaid by
himself, Ahl-lil had a stallion to match.

From woods and gullies and waste places their vast
herds of pigs were taken in. They were measured and
matched and noted. And Mayve had one fine boar, but
Ahl-lil had another just as fine.

Then their droves and free-wandering cattle from the
woods and wastes of the province were brought in.
These were matched and measured and noted also, and
found to be the same in number and size. But . . . but!
There was one great bull in Ahl-lil's herd that had been
a calf of one of Mayve's cows – Finnvenock, the White
Horned, was his name. And Finnvenock, refusing to be
led by a woman, had gone over to the king's herd.
Mayve couldn't find in her herd the equal of this bull,
and her spirits drooped as though she owned not one
small thing at all.

Mayve had the chief messenger of Ireland called. Mac
Roth was his name, and she told him to see where the
match of the White Horned might be found in any
province of Ireland.

"I already know where to find such a bull and better," Mac Roth said. "In the province of Ulster, in the territory of Coolee, in Daire Mac Feeockna's house. Don Coolee is the bull's name, the Brown Bull of Coolee."

"Go there, Mac Roth," Mayve said. "Ask Daire to lend me Don Coolee for a year. At the end of the year, he can have fifty yearling heifers in payment for the loan, and the Brown Bull of Coolee back again. And you can offer him this too, Mac Roth, if the people of his country think badly of losing their fine jewel: if Daire himself comes with the bull I'll give him a portion of the fine Plain of Ai, equal to his own lands, and a one-of-a-kind chariot, cunningly made of wicker and copper. And my own friendly thighs on top of that."

Messengers set out for Daire Mac Feeockna's house: there were nine of them with Mac Roth. Mac Roth was soon made welcome in Daire's house, as befitted Ireland's chief messenger. Daire asked him what brought him to Ulster and the territory of Coolee, and the chief messenger told him why he came, and about the pillow talk between Mayve and Ahl-lil.

"So I am here to ask about the loan of the Don Coolee, to match against Finnvenock," he said. "And you'll get fifty yearling heifers back in payment for the loan, and Don Coolee himself, and more besides. If you come with the bull yourself, you'll get a portion of the

Plain of Ai, equal to your own lands, and a certain chariot worth more than thrice seven bondsmaids, and Mayve's friendly thighs on top of it all."

Daire so jumped for joy that the seams in his cushion burst under him, and he cried, "True as my soul, I don't care what the Ulstermen think. Don Coolee is my treasure to do what I want with. I'll take the Don Coolee to Mayve and Ahl-lil in the land of Connaught."

Mac Roth was pleased at Mac Feeockna's decision. He and his men were being well looked after. Rushes and fresh straw were settled under them, and they were given the best of good food. Needless to say, they were kept well supplied with liquor, so they grew drunk and noisy.

Two of the messengers were talking. One of them said, "There's no doubt the man of the house here is a good man."

"A good man, certainly," a second man said.

First: "Is there a better man in Ulster?"

Second: "There is, certainly. His leader Conckovor is a better man. If the whole of Ulster gave in to him, it would be no shame for them. Anyway, it was good of Mac Feeockna to give us the Don Coolee. It would have taken four strong provinces of Ireland to carry him off otherwise."

A third man joined the talk. "What are you arguing about?" he asked.

Second man: "This messenger just said, 'Daire Mac Feeockna is a good man,' and I said, 'A good man certainly.'"

First man: "And I said, 'Is there a better man in Ulster?'"

Second man: "To which I answered, 'His leader, Conckovor, the King of Ulster, is a better man. If the whole of Ulster gave into him, it would be no shame. But even so, and I'll say it again, it was good of Daire Mac Feeockna to give us what we asked for. Otherwise, four strong provinces of Ireland would be needed to take such a treasure from Ulster.'"

Third man: "May the mouth that said that spout blood! We would have taken it away anyway, with or without Daire's leave."

At that moment the man in charge of Daire Mac Feeockna's household came into the hut, with a man carrying drink and another man with food. When he heard what the messengers were saying, he was seized with fury. He slammed down their food and drink, saying neither "Eat!" nor "Don't eat!"

He went straight to Daire Mac Feeockna's hut and demanded, "Did you give our famous treasure, the Don Coolee, to Mayve's messengers?"

"Yes, I did," Daire said.

"That was not a kingly thing to do. What they said is

true: if you hadn't given him up freely, the hosts of Ahl-lil and Mayve, abetted by the battle wisdom of Ferzus, would have had him without your leave."

"By the gods I worship, nothing leaves here unless I choose to let it!"

They waited. They waited till morning. The messengers got up early the next day and went to Daire's hut. "Tell us, sir, where to find the Don Coolee."

"I will not," Daire said. "And only it isn't my habit to murder messengers or travelers or any other wayfarers, not one of you would leave here alive."

"Why is this?" asked Mac Roth.

"For a good reason," Daire said. "You said if I didn't give willingly, the hosts of Mayve and Ahl-lil would make me give. And they be advised by the ancient warrior Ferzus!"

"Indeed," Mac Roth said, "what messengers say into their cups hardly deserves your notice. You can't blame Ahl-lil and Mayve."

"Still, I won't give up my bull this time, Mac Roth, not as long as I can help it."

So the messengers set off again, and came to Crooahnee, the stronghold of Connaught. Mayve asked them for the news and Mac Roth said Daire wouldn't give up his bull.

"Why not?" Mayve asked.

Mac Roth told what had happened.

"We needn't polish every knob and knot in this," Mayve said. "It is well known that the Brown Bull of Coolee would be taken by force if it was not given freely."

And oh, my dears! From that talk upon the pillow sprang all the troubles of Ireland.

THE ROMAN EMPEROR
AND THE WELSH PRINCESS

axen was Emperor of Rome, and he was more handsome and wiser than any who went before him, and better suited to be emperor. One day he summoned an assembly of kings and said, "I wish to go hunting tomorrow." Early in the morning, he set out with his companions, to the valley of a river that runs down toward Rome. They hunted the valley until midday. And well for you to know, there were two-and-thirty crowned kings in that company, his vassals all. Not for the joy of hunting did the emperor hunt with them so long, but because he had been made a man of such high dignity that it behooved him to show his lordship whilst engaged in the most ancient of pastimes, the art of the chase.

By noon the sun was high in the heavens and the heat of the valley great. Maxen found himself being

overcome with sleep and ordered a respite. A chamberlain placed a golden shield beneath his head, and other
chamberlains grouped themselves around him to make a
sort of castle of spears and shields to shelter him in
shadow. And these chamberlains, all, were crowned
kings, who counted themselves as honored to stand
guard over Maxen and protect him from the rays of the
noontime sun. In this wise, the emperor slept.

And as he slept he dreamed. He saw himself traveling
through the valley and reaching the highest mountain
in the world – it seemed as high as the sky. Having
crossed this mountain he saw himself traversing a grand
plain, the loveliest land that anyone had ever seen.
Broad rivers flowed down from the mountains to the sea,
and he made along these rivers to their outlets, and
though his journey was long he finally reached the
mouth of the mightiest river anyone had seen. There he
saw a great city, and a great fortress, within which were
many tall towers of different colors, and the greatest
fleet he had ever seen. One of the ships was much bigger
and more beautiful than any of the others. In as far as
he could see that part that was above the water, alter-
nating, one plank was of gold and another of silver. A
bridge of ivory led from the ship to the shore, and
Maxen saw himself crossing that bridge, whereupon the
sail was hoisted and the ship set out to cross the sea.

In no time at all the ship came to the most beautiful island in the world. Maxen crossed that island, from one sea to another, to the very farthest reaches. He saw steep slopes and high crags and a harsh rough land whose like he had never seen before. Beyond it was an island in the sea, but between where he stood on the mountain, and where was the island, he saw a plain as broad as the sea that separated the island from the land, and a forest that was as wide as the mountain where he stood. From this mountain a river ran through the land and down to the sea, and at the mouth of the river stood a handsome fortress. The gate was open and he entered.

Inside, Maxen saw a fine hall: its roof seemed all of gold, its sides of luminous stones all equally precious, its door all of gold. There were golden couches and silver tables, and on the couch, facing him, were two auburn-haired youths playing a board game in which one side's king was attempting to escape to the edge of the board, and the other side was attempting to capture him. The board was made up of squares, alternate silver and gold, and the men were of gold and silver, too. And in his dream, Maxen knew that he knew the name of that game: gwyddbwyll; and what's more, he knew how to pronounce it: g'thvyll. (But only in his dream!)

The two lads were dressed in pure black brocade, with headbands of red gold restraining their hair, and rubies

and gems and imperial stones were set into the bands, in
alternation. And these lads wore shoes of finest
Cordovan leather, held fast by golden straps. By the base
of the pillar, Maxen saw a white-haired man sitting in a
chair of elephant ivory, to which was affixed an image of
two Roman eagles in red gold. On his snowy head was a
crown of gold, and he wore gold armlets and rings, and
there was a gold torque around his neck. But it was not
the gold that gave him an air of distinction; he was of
such aristocratic mien as to be impressive in his own
right. A checkered board, for playing g'thvyll, lay before
him, and in his hands a bar of gold and a file; he was
fashioning men for the game.

Maxen also saw a girl; she was sitting near the aged
man in a chair of red gold. Looking at the sun at its
most dazzling would be no harder than looking at her
beauty. She wore shifts of white silk with red gold fas-
tenings across the breast, and a gold belt around her
slender waist. She wore a surcoat of gold brocade and a
gold mantle, which was fastened with a brooch of red
gold. Her hairband was studded with rubies and other
gems and pearls. She was the loveliest sight a man could
ever see. From her golden chair she rose to greet Maxen.
She held out her arms to him, and he threw his arms
around her neck, and they sat down upon the chair.
And lo! That chair was as comfortable for two, sitting

close together, as it had been for her alone. Both his arms were around her, and they were sitting cheek to cheek, but . . . but . . . What with the hounds straining at their leashes, and the edges of the shields banging together, and the spear shafts rubbing together, and the stamping and whinnying of the horses, the emperor woke up.

When Maxen woke there was no life or being or existence in him because of the girl he had seen in his dream. Not a knucklebone, not the tip of a fingernail, let alone anything more, was not full of love for her. His retainers said, "Lord, it is past your mealtime, the chefs will be waiting for us." So the emperor, the saddest man ever seen, mounted his palfrey and rode back to Rome, and thus he remained for a week, refusing to eat. When his entourage went to drink wine and mead from golden cups, he stayed behind; when they went to listen to songs and stories, and watch entertainments, he stayed behind. He did nothing but sleep, for then he would dream of the woman he loved best, and when he was awake he cared for nothing because he did not know where she was or how he could find her.

One day a chamberlain spoke to him (though he was a chamberlain, he was also King of Romani), "Lord, your courtiers slander you."

"Why should they be doing so?"

"Because you do not speak to us nor share yourself with us. You give neither the counsel nor cheer nor orders that men expect from their lord."

Maxen sighed, but he bestirred himself. "Summon the wise men of Rome and I will tell them why I am so melancholy." The wise men gathered and Maxen told them, "I have had a dream, and in that dream I have seen a girl, and because of her there is not life nor being nor existence in me."

The wise men consulted among themselves, then their leader said, "Lord, as you have asked us, we will advise you. For the next three years send messengers to the three parts of the earth in search of your dream. Since you will never know at what time of day or night good news might arrive, that much hope will sustain you in your duties and your life." Messengers were sent to roam the world, seeking news of the emperor's dream, but when they returned at the end of a year they knew no more than when they had set out, and the emperor was saddened more, thinking he would never hear news of the woman he loved.

Then the King of the Romani said, "Lord, go back to that place where you saw yourself in your dream, either east or west." The emperor followed his suggestion. He found the riverbank and said, "This is where I was in my dream, and I was moving westward, upstream." Thirteen

men set out as the emperor's messengers, and this is how
they were dressed: each one wore the empty sleeve of
his cloak in front of him as a sign that he was a messenger, so they would come to no harm when passing
through warring lands. Thus they journeyed until they
saw before them an alpine wall made up of many mountains; the tallest of them was white-horned and seemed
to meet the sky. Having crossed the mountains, they
came to a broadly expansive plain through which rivers
flowed, and they said, "Look, here is the land that our
lord described to us." Then they came to the mightiest
of rivers, to which the others were mere branches, and
they followed it to the sea. At the mouth of that river
there was a great city, and a fortress with towers of many
hues and colors, and a port where was gathered the
greatest fleet in the world. They said to one another,
"So it all is, as in our Emperor Maxen's dream."

One ship was larger than the others; the messengers
would hardly have been amazed if its planks had been
gold and silver. They boarded and sailed to the fairest
isle in all the world, the Isle of Britain. And they journeyed across Britain until they came to a place of harsh
slopes and steep crags, which was then called Eryri, but
is now called Snowdon. "Here is the very same our lord
did dream," they said. From the heights of Snowdon
they espied a plain, and that plain was Arvon, and

beyond the plain the sea, and an island offshore; that
island was once called Mon, but now is Anglesey. A
river descended through the plain, and where it opened
to the sea, an estuary, called Aber Seint; commanding
the estuary, a Roman fort, Segontium. Finding the gate
open, they entered a great hall. They turned to each
other and said, "This is surely the hall that our lord saw
in his dream."

Within the hall they saw two youths, clad in black
brocade, sitting on a golden couch and playing a board
game. They saw a white-haired king in an ivory chair at
the base of a marble column; he was carving miniature
figures of kings and horsemen and foot soldiers out of a
bar of gold. But it was when the messengers saw the
most beautiful woman in the world sitting in a chair of
red gold, next to the old man, that they knew without
doubt they had arrived at the place their lord had
dreamed. They knelt down before the young woman
and hailed her as Empress of Rome.

"Sirs," she said, "you have the look of noblemen, as
well as the badge of messengers. Why then do you
mock me?"

"Lady, we do not. The Emperor of Rome has seen you
in a dream and now joy and duty, even the willingness
to exist, have left him. We give you a choice: you may

come with us and be made empress in Rome, or else the emperor will come here to make you his wife."

"Messengers," she answered, "I do not doubt that you believe what you say, but I do not believe what you say overmuch. If it is I whom the emperor loves, let him come for me."

The messengers rode day and night to return to Rome. When their horses failed them, they bought new ones. Upon arriving they went immediately to the emperor and asked for their reward, which they got even as they were asking. "Lord, we will guide you by land and sea to the woman you love best. We know who she is and where she can be found in the real world, not only in a dream. Her name is Helen, and she is the daughter of King Eudav, son of Caradawg, of Wales. We know her father's royal lineage, and we know her mother's too, for among the Britons, the female blood-line is more important than the male."

At once the emperor and his host set out, taking the messengers along as guides. Up the valley and over the Alps they went, and down to the sea. They sailed to the Isle of Britain and crossed the isle to Snowdon, and descended from the heights to the plain of Arvon, where stood the fortress of Segontium. The emperor recognized it immediately as the castle in his dream.

Maxen entered the fortress, and inside the hall he saw the two auburn-haired princes, Kynan and Adeon, each clad in black brocade; each with a gold coronet on his brow. They were still playing g'thvyll. Their royal father, white-haired Eudav, son of Caradawg, sat by a pillar, fashioning golden figures for the game. Beside him, the girl in Maxen's dream, the woman he loved most in the world, was sitting in a red gold chair, and she was more beautiful than ever. "Hail to the Empress of Rome," he said and went to embrace her.

That night, he slept with her. The next morning she asked for her bride-gift, for he had found her a virgin, and he told her to name her own gift. For herself, as Empress of Rome, she asked for the offshore islands of Britain: the isles of Wight, of Man, of Anglesey, and the Orkneys. She asked for the Isle of Britain for her father, from the English Channel to the Irish Sea, but she reserved for herself the right to choose three fortresses of Britain. She chose Arvon, and Caerleon, and Camaerthon, and thought to have stone highways built across Britain, from one fortress to another. The hosts of Wales flocked to build such roads, which are now called the Highways of Helen of the Hosts, because for no one else would free-born Welshmen have done such back-breaking and exacting work of their own will. She asked that the chief fortress be built at Arvon, and she sent ships to Rome, to return with ballasts of Roman earth, so that her husband, the emperor, could sit and sleep and move about in his own native element, and thus remain happy and healthy.

Maxen spent seven years in Britain. At that time it was the custom of the Romans that whenever an emperor stayed conquering in another land for seven years, he must stay abroad and not be allowed to return to Rome. A new emperor was elected, and he sent to Maxen a threatening letter, no more than this: *If you come to Rome, and if you ever come!* The letter came to Maxen while he was at the headquarters of the Roman legions, at Caerleon-on-Usk, and he sent a letter to the man who was claiming to be emperor, no more than this: *And if I go to Rome, and if I go!* Then Maxen and his host set out for Rome. On the way he conquered France and Burgundy, and then he laid siege to Rome, but after a year he was no closer to taking the city than he had been the first day, for the walls were high and well built and the new emperor had assembled a mighty army that, although besieged, could not be overcome.

Then came news that Helen's brothers, Kynan and Adeon, had arrived from Britain and were approaching Rome. Maxen and Helen marched out to meet them. The British host was small in number, but each Briton was worth two Romans in skill and fierceness and cunning; moreover, their two Welsh princes had been playing g'thvyll for years. Indeed, Kynan and Adeon observed the scene as though they were scanning the pieces on a game board, and noted that every day at noon the two armies stopped all hostilities for several hours while each of the two contending emperors enjoyed his noon-day meal. Kynan said to Adeon, "Lest we forget how to play, what say you, brother, to a quick, short game during dinner break?" And Adeon replied, "Always keep in mind, dear brother, how a few clever moves can drive a rival off the edge of the board."

And so, by night, they sent men secretly to measure the height of the walls of Rome, and then they set their men to making wooden ladders, one ladder to every four men in their army. And when the ladders were made, they laid their plans. Therefore, at the very time when an assault was least expected, and the Romans were eating and drinking with their respective emperors, the men of Britain, led by Kynan and Adeon, set their ladders against the walls of the city and entered Rome. Before the new emperor had time to arm himself and fight, the Welsh fell upon him and slew him, along with his bodyguard and the most prestigious of his followers. For three days and three nights they fought in the streets and the houses of the city. Meanwhile, warriors were set to guard the gates so none could escape; nor might any man come in.

News of the attack came to the Emperor Maxen, but no news came directly from Kynan or Adeon. After three days, Maxen said to Helen, "It is strange that I have had no word from your brothers, neither asking for help nor telling whether they have succeeded or failed."

"Lord," said Helen, "my brothers are the wisest young men in the world: they will not have failed. They will have taken Rome for you. Go to the gates, and they will give up the city to you." So Maxen and Helen went to the gates of Rome and the gates were opened to them, and Maxen went to his palace and sat upon his throne once more. And all this was due to the men of Britain. To Kynan and Adeon, Maxen gave his whole army, that they might conquer lands for themselves; and this they did until they were wearied of conquests. Kynan laid down his sword to rule the lands that he had won, but Adeon yearned for his own country and so returned to the Isle of Britain.

Maxen and Helen ruled in Rome, and in their time was prosperity and contentment.

TRISTAN HERO

hen Tristan returned from Lyonesse, he found King Mark and all his court in mourning, for the King of Ireland had manned a fleet to ravage Cornwall. For fifteen years, King Mark had refused to pay a tribute tax that his father and his father's father before him had paid.

My listeners, to fully appreciate this tale you should know that certain old treaties gave the men of Ireland the right to levy on the men of Cornwall a heavy burden: one year, three hundred pounds of copper; the next year, three hundred pounds of silver; the third year, three hundred pounds of gold. And the fourth year? Ah, the fourth year will break your heart, for the Irish might take with them three hundred youths and three hundred maidens, chosen by lot from among the Cornish folk.

Now this particular year the Irish king had sent, to carry out the treaty, his wife's own brother, the Morholt, a knight of giant stature. His very name meant "death-dealer": no man yet had overcome him. By the time Tristan arrived from overseas, King Mark had already summoned his barons to Castle Dore, above the port of Foy, to hear the Morholt speak. On the day of reckoning, the king's council gathered, and when the king had taken his throne, the Morholt said:

"King Mark, the King of Ireland arraigns you to pay at last what you have owed so long, and because you have refused too long already, he bids you this day to give over three hundred youths and three hundred maidens drawn by lot from among the Cornish folk. My ships, anchored in Foy estuary, will bear them away that they may become our slaves. Nevertheless, if any one of your barons would prove by trial of combat that the King of Ireland receives this tribute without right, I will take up his wager. Of course, as is meet, you, King Mark, are excepted. Even so, which among you, my Cornish lords, will fight to redeem this land?"

The barons glanced at each other out of the corners of their eyes. No one spoke aloud, but this one said to himself: "Behold the stature of the Morholt. He is stronger than four robust men. Should I court death? Tempt God? Rather, thank God, that I am not a mad man, bent on the impossible." That one, to himself: "Behold the Morholt's sword! As though by magic it has struck off the heads of the bravest champions in all the years since the King of Ireland has sent his death-dealer among the vassal lands. It would be suicide to go against him. And that would be a sin." Another: "Is it to become slaves that I have reared you, my dear sons, and you, my dear daughters, to become harlots? But my death would not save you." And all remained silent, like sparrows put into a cage with a hawk.

Again the Morholt spoke, "Lords of Cornwall, which among you accepts my challenge? I offer him a noble battle. Three days hence we will go by boats to the islet of Saint Sampson, in the offing of this port. There your champion and I will fight in single combat; even though I kill him, the glory of the battle will honor all his kin."

Silence.

For the third time, the Morholt spoke, "Very well, rare Cornish lords, since this course seems the nobler to you: draw your children by lot that I may bear them away. But I did not think this land was inhabited by serfs only."

Then Tristan knelt at the feet of King Mark and said, "Lord King, by your leave I will do battle." And in vain would King Mark have turned him from his purpose, thinking, how could even valor save so young a knight?

But he threw down his gage to the Morholt, and the Morholt took up the gage.

On the day appointed, Tristan had himself clad in chain mail and helm. The barons wept for pity of the youthful knight and for shame of themselves. The bells pealed, and all, those of the nobility and those of low degree, old men and children and women, weeping and praying, escorted Tristan to the shore. Hope still stirred in their hearts, for hope still springs on lean pastures.

Tristan took the tiller of his little boat and headed out from shore, bound for the islet of Saint Sampson. There the knights were to fight, each to each. Alone! Now the Morholt had hoisted to his mast a sail of rich purple and, coming fast to land, he moored his vessel on the shore. But Tristan gave his own boat a good kick and set it adrift.

"Vassal, what are you doing?" asked the Morholt. "Why didn't you fasten your boat with a mooring line as I have done?"

"Vassal, why should I?" Tristan answered. "Only one of us will go hence alive. One boat will suffice."

And each rousing the other to the fray, they passed into the middle of the isle. No man saw the sharp combat, but thrice the salt sea breeze wafted a cry of fury to the land. The Cornish women standing on the shore beat their palms in chorus, in sign of mourning.

Massed to one side before their tent, the companions of the Morholt laughed at them.

Then, toward the hour of noon, the purple sail showed far off; the Irish boat appeared from the island shore, and the women raised a clamor of distress: "The Morholt" The Morholt! When suddenly, as the boat grew larger on the sight and topped a wave, they saw a knight standing at its prow. Each of his hands brandished a sword.

It was Tristan!

Immediately twenty boats launched forth while youths and maidens swam out to meet him. The good knight leapt ashore, and as the mothers kissed the steel upon his feet he cried to the Morholt's men, "My lords of Ireland, the Morholt fought well. See? My sword is broken and a splinter of it stands fast in his head. Take you the splinter, my lords. That steel is the tribute of Cornwall!"

Then the Cornish youths, rejoicing, lifted Tristan to their shoulders and went up the steep streets of Foy, toward Castle Dore. As they went, the people he had freed waved green boughs. Banners and rich cloths were hung from the windows, while all around, a jubilation, a pealing of bells, a sounding of horns and trumpets so lusty that one could not have heard God had He thundered; but when they reached the castle the victorious knight drooped in the arms of King Mark. Blood ran from his wounds.

The Morholt's men landed in Ireland, quite downcast. For whenever he came back to his home port, the Morholt had been wont to take joy in the sight of his clan upon the shore, of the queen, his sister, and of his niece, Iseult the Fair, the golden-haired, whose beauty already shone like the breaking dawn. Tenderly had they cherished him, and if he had taken a wound they healed him, for they were skilled in alms and potions. But now their magic was in vain, for he lay dead.

Dead! And sewn in a deer hide. A piece of the foreign brand yet stood in his skull, till Iseult plucked it out and shut it in an ivory coffer. The niece of the Morholt revered that precious splinter as she would a saint's bone.

Bowed over the tall corpse, mother and daughter ceaselessly repeated the praises of the dead man, ceaselessly hurled imprecations at the murderer, and by turns led the women in the funeral dirge. From that day forward, Iseult the Fair knew and hated the name of Tristan of Lyonesse.

But over at Castle Dore, Tristan languished, for a poisonous blood trickled from his wound. The doctors found that the Morholt had thrust into him a poisoned barb, and since their potions and theriac could never heal him, they withdrew their ministrations and left

him in God's hands. So hateful a stench came from the
wound that all his dearest friends fled him, all save his
uncle, King Mark, and his old squire, Gorvenal. They
always could stay near him because their love overcame
their abhorrence.

At last Tristan had himself carried into a hut, set apart
upon the shore. Lying there, facing the sea, he awaited
death. He thought, "I know, fair uncle, that you would
give your life for mine; and you also, dear Gorvenal. But
what availeth tenderness? I still must die. Yet my heart is
lifted as I lie here in the sun. Now I would like to try the
sea. Yes! I would have the sea bear me far off alone, to
what land no matter, just so it heal me of my wound.
Perhaps, dear uncle, I will once more serve you – as your
harper and your huntsman and your liege.

He begged so long that those two who loved him
most accepted his desire. They bore him into a boat
with neither sail nor oar nor sword. His harp only his
uncle placed beside him, for sail he could not lift nor oar
ply nor sword wield. As a sailor on some long voyage
casts off to sea a beloved shipmate dead, so Gorvenal
pushed out to sea that boat where his dear Tristan lay.
And the sea pulled him away.

For seven days and seven nights, the sea drew him.
At times, to charm his grief, he harped. At last, when
the sea brought him near another shore where

fishermen had left their port that night to fish far out.
As they rowed they heard a sweet and strong and
living tune that ran above the sea; feathering their
oars, they listened.

In the first light of the dawn they saw the boat at
large. As they rowed, they shared among themselves
stories of Saint Brennan, whose ship, surrounded by
supernatural music, sailed westward over a sea as white
as milk. They directed themselves toward the boat,
although she went here and there at random. Nothing
seemed to live in her except the sound of the harp. But
as they neared, the airy tune grew weak and died. Just as
they pulled athwart, Tristan's hand fell lifeless on the
strings, although the strings still trembled.

EPILOGUE

And the strings still trembled."

SOURCES

Bedier, Joseph. *The Romance of Tristan and Iseult.*
Translated by Hilaire Belloc and completed by Paul
Rosenfeld. Pantheon Books, 1945

Cahill, Thomas. *How the Irish Saved Civilization: The
Untold Story of Ireland's Heroic Role from the Fall of Rome
to the Rise of Medieval Europe.* London: Hodder &
Stoughton, 1995.

Gantz, Jeffrey, translator. *The Mabinogion.* Markham,
Ontario: Penguin, 1976.

Jackson, Kenneth Hurlstone, editor and translator. *A
Celtic Miscellany: Translations from the Celtic Literatures.*
London: Routledge & Paul, 1951.

Jacobs, Joseph. *English Fairy Tales*. London: David Nutt, 1890.

Jacobs, Joseph. *More English Fairy Tales*. London: David Nutt, 1894.

Jones, Gwyn, and Thomas Jones, translators. *The Mabinogion*. London: Everyman's Library, 1949.

Kinsella, Thomas, translator. *The Tain: Translated from the Irish Epic Tain bo Cuailnge*. London, New York: Oxford University Press, 1970.

Picard, Barbara Leonie. *Tales of the British People*. Criterion Books, 1961.

Schreiber, Charlotte, Lady. *The Mabinogion: From the Welsh of the Llyfr coch o Hergest in the Library of Jesus College, Oxford*. Translated by Lady Charlotte Guest. Cardiff: J. Jones Cardiff, 1977.